To Carney -
Solidarity and friendship

[signature] 2003

The Neverfield

Library of Congress Cataloging-in-Publication Data

Handal, Nathalie, 1969-
Never*field* poem / Nathalie Handal.
p. cm.
ISBN 0-942996-35-6 (alk. paper)
I. Title
PS3558. A4625N48 1999
811'. 54—dc21   99-12232
                                                             CIP

Cover and book design by The Set Up, London

The Post-Apollo Press
35 Marie Street
Sausalito, California 94965

Printed in the United States of America on acid-free paper.

The Neverfield

Nathalie Handal

THE POST-APOLLO PRESS
Sausalito, California

To My Grandmothers
To My Parents

Derrière les décors
De l' existence immense, au plus noir de l' abîme,
Je vois distinctement des mondes singuliers,
Et... la voix me console et dit: "Garde tes songes;
Les sages n' en ont pas d' aussi beaux que les fous!"

            – Charles Baudelaire

I...
Fold and unfold my wings

Perform the rites in my field
In my beak I transform
A dewdrop and a grain of earth into song

       – Vasko Popa

the yellow branch kneeled in front of my crying feet,
the field's elevating fingers seized the sunlight,
nothing else existed but yellow
yellow
was I ever to see more?

"Much is in the blood... because the blood has memory, memory that has been imprinted, encoded, from the past – the whispers of the blood are stories. The rational mind works in tandem with that information; in fact, its job is to bring that to light, to tell us who we are."

– Rudolfo Anaya

Decades of riding through skies wearing different costumes, landing
in squares strange to the heart, feeling like a misplaced light in a
dying day, like a phantom passing through a village with no one to
observe...
feeling like a spy exposed myself as the tongue speaks everything
with a foreign tone, continuously spinning around the wounded
moon...
feeling abandoned inside the darkest room of myself, knowing that
all the openings are open but none are
mine...
later

after stopping in many stations
the mind holds on to one flight –
when
it is not
the language my mouth speaks,
nor the landscape my face reflects,

but
the name I carry,
the murmuring of my blood
that
is
my only claim
the only one that really matters...

my mind leaves to remember...

in the yellowness of my life
I met the crowd of my memory
saw the face on a fig leaf
found the name of the pearl
forgot the gloom
in the dune's mouth...   and remembered

a childhood of moving streetlights,
changing eyes as the night's color shifted moods,
as belonging became deaf, as my mind accompanied
the sailboats across earth's heart while longing for a
corner in my grandfather's blood, while waiting
for the suitcase to retire,
the olive groves to expand...   expand

in that place where the grain of my veins
was first harvested,
that place where oranges stopped us from starving
and dust painted itself on our bare breasts...
women
of that place
awoke day after day
polishing the fragmented lamps
and the invisible doorknobs,
sitting under the only almond tree
reciting a prophesy heavier than
the moon's mind...
losing their features
in their backyards
but owning a single coat
large enough to warm
the entire village...   and I

weightless, stumbled out of insomnia
into a dream
which was dreamless...

all forgotten
in a vapor long evaporated
all –
caged in a burnt feather...
but when stones stopped choking
and became trumpets on fire...   it was I

who let the cities loose
and kept the graffiti on the walls,
it was I who took the last poster
of the town before and gave it
to my dead neighbor who fought for it
all of his life...
it was I, who was I but the reflection
of a people imprisoned in a picture...

      the reflection

of yellow clouds settled inside of me
like bedouins who had found their evening spot...
I peeled the thoughts from my mind
and moved to Alexandria
where I saw the praying flutes
and found the unknown thought of a Sufi...
at that time bowls only kept
the glittering dew
and I was still riding
on an unnamed horse,   still

observing flakes transforming into daisies
at the end of a Boston afternoon,
still watching straws trapping
hummingbirds
and the Diva capturing them both...
and it was in those nights in Bloomsbury
when the breeze was what
kept the candlelights illuminated
that I heard the shepherd's voice...   that

I remembered picking the tulips which grew
on your tongue...
rolling for hours
days
in a landscape of carnation leaves...
I would put mint syrup all over my body
the cigar's fog always hid us
from all which aimed to hunt us down...
but the sombre maze
held us captive
and
you had to hide between the years
I would never have the time to arrive to...

a drop of your liquor remained
on the lines of my neck   and I

waited,
waited
for a verdict long pronounced,
long resting in the sand's horn
somewhere
in Jordan's
irretrievable desert
foams of nostalgia
covered my womb,
a lonely violin awoke the tempest,
giant flames captured
my ultimate farewel   and

Lancelot appeared
before the jury of rocks...
the lace veils of tortured widows started humming
the sacrificed
       was
 sa cri fi ced...   and

I stood on top of the theatre's
mountain of applauding hands
revolted –
all froze...
perhaps I could have rewritten the scene,
but did I have the right to change
the handwriting of His scriptures...
I left...   left

and looked for the poet who wrote

"Towards my heart,
The only town not captured yet."

the poet who wrote lines
which entered my silence
        and
        did
          not disturb the birds...

the poet I saw once...
but whose words have long been
windows of invincible candles...

perhaps
when we will no longer be trapped
between life and living,
when we will be riding the train to
where stones are building fountains,
perhaps
then
I will find the poet...

I know he will own
the last sight of the battle
and he will write the last
very last
poem of the world...
I continue looking for the poet
who stands at the end of the yellow field...
I know the poet...
I am really looking
            for the man...

heard the field singing
but couldn't hear the words,
saw the leaves dancing
but couldn't see the moves...

I

walked
walked
walked
until walking died
and I flew

        into

            yellow's mouth...

the heath was gone
the wintergreen was gone
the blueberry stain on my skirt was gone...   gone

like the images of forgotten photos
strolling between the hay rolls during springtime
but regaining their place in the back of an
abandoned drawer when snow ruled the heavens...

gone like those moments when
I imagined kufiyahs
filling the silver midnight,
imagined villagers imagining flower petals
surrounding their houses,
imagined dryness settling on thousands of lips
and girls dyeing their mothers' dresses
hoping it would pass unnoticed...

and where were the birds when we needed them?

heard the cries of betrayed souls in the country
between here and nowhere
the crashing of waves against cracked corpses,
the barrels' swords preparing a war against their
burning minds,
and silence's
echo
lost
in
the
corner
of
a
soldier's
memory...   and

grief sat on the peasants' hair
wrinkled faces haunted their sleep
even as they
dreamt of jade
and ribbons of cinnamon...
the children
saw the needle staircases...   the

bitter thorns that grew on the ox's head,
the tyrant's invading jungle,
the bald fighter's single arm,
the
enraged
tribes
disputing
over
the last crumb...   and

if I were a woman
who didn't know she had colors
on the palette of her stomach,
if I were a woman
with a naked mind
               and
                    an empty eye...

then they could have unknotted my braids in my hair
and sent me across the border...

but the field continued growing
our forefathers' names

                    our grandmothers' traits...

my cousin's auburn hair continued sending
messages to tents she couldn't see,
continued saying that
the blue leaves would one day be green again,
                    continued

hearing the bells singing
from Prague's forgotten window...
was this the Eternal Wake?
my eyes remained opened even as they closed,
faces appeared on the rocks of my dream,
Armenian Duduk came from over there...
                    I
                walked until
                 the fog
          lost itself in my eyes...

the sage in my life appeared before me
                                              and

as all disappeared with modern hands...

I watched him

standing on

a floating cloud of incense

eyes closed

speaking

in the divine language

becoming

the

single

unicorn...

I wanted to forget

so

as the stranded scarecrow
commanded the windmills
to sweep away the haze...
I commanded myself to sweep away the memories
which slept under the scented cedar
curtain brought back
from over there...   slowly

the image of a man's back
appeared on the wall of my eyes...
his grey hair seduced
by the endless drums,
his muscles fighting
the furious speech...
he seemed like the
captain in my other life
but
never did I see his face
for copper clouds
kept him under their armpits...   you

I felt you browsing through my mind...
and warned you that
the republic inside of you
might
          tumble
                    down
                              your
                                        chest...
warned you
not to go near the notebooks
piled up by the cup of tea
                              and the half-moon.
but go beside the clay sculpture
by the pinewood...
I heard the march of the patriots
you read the notebooks...   I

stood in the middle
of dying and death...

to move toward the idols
would be to abandon my flesh,
to go back to yards of disputing wires
would be never to have
       known
that doves wear indigo scarves...

I felt like a tortured leaf,
but the words of the poet
conquered pain's sword stabbing my mind...

I cried, simply cried
knowing I would touch the first olive tree
with his hands,
knowing that the house at the far point of our lives
would be yellow...   and I

loved the dreamlike passage
in his eyes,
loved love's
nude pastures and humble hay fields,
the way love's fingers
tenderly touched the fountain's birthmark...

did we see the same deer?

the jug of wine
the kiss of madness
the quiet love
carried by our distant shoulders
the jar of butterflies
the map we covered ourselves with
while dreaming of golden beads...
I hid his stares
in the secret lines of my dress
and loved his aging hands...

"... let us go out into the fields

and spend the night in villages.

Let us wake early and go to the vineyards

and see if the vine is in blossom."

II

When I started walking through the field
my eyes were blue
continued walking
my eyes turned grey...
I wrote to the field
continued writing
no letter arrived...

I threw a yellow outcry
the field never even sighed...

in the never field

I continued walking
then turned...   saw

watermelons holding the kite up
as the native slept under the mango tree,
saw plantations and plantations of dancers
waiting to hear the crops' wisdom...
and
as night walked in
from the hillsides
I saw so many vidas
dipping themselves in apricot jam
waiting
for the mild hurricane
to wash away
past grass
and
turn
everything green...   waiting

for puddles of mud
to turn into
cascades of sapphires and diamonds...

the Caribbean's torrid soil had a way
to play with minds,
carrying people behind the sun
where thoughts had graceful walks
and nothing really mattered but
the mangrove's shade...

                    I

an endless observer of the river baths,
listened to the water's legend
and its never ending wishes...
watched the witch's potion
in
every
drop
of the river...   as night slept

I traveled inside a house
I onced belonged to...
the kitchen table kept
my Sitti's expression sealed on its wooden surface,
the reflection of familiar faces crowded the pale ceiling
and my heart fled
to a shade somewhere shades had been exiled...
I thought of my father's falling eyes
as they spoke of sand shadows,
carrying him to the origins of his name...

I heard the weeping of a gazelle
        inside
            a man
        living
            between
        two walls...

as all the arabesque cushions
lined themselves on the long stretched sofa
I knew my mother was there...

the pine trees found
the passageway through the enchantress's hair
and we had all reached the dome...
I looked towards my brother
grains of rice embraced him
as he became tomorrow's knight
and we had all reached the dome...

and I,

during amber nights
on the tip of my toes,
entered his mind's woodland,
soaked my feet in the river behind the last tree,
kidnapped the poems he hadn't written yet
and hid them in my throbbing wrist...
went in his crescent heart
took all of his love
and hid it...

all was hazy...
I sat on the only log in this woody country
when finally I found a talisman in the wind's breath
and left for my world of spices and escaping ink...

only later realizing that
I had forgotten the harp
that told the date the poet's secrets,
the coffee beans
that gave him a voice,
the sap of the maple tree
that gave his hands light...
his footprints were all over my body...
was it love witnessing its awakening
or were we simply poets?   I

left for Picasso's blue period
to find my sister...

bluebells covering our stripped bodies...
coins dominating the sky, singing to us,
like miniature bells...
"Sister, where have you put the Damascus sky?
You must not keep it for too long,
you might forget that you've placed it
on the tip of your eyes..."

a bluebell's feathered pen started writing
on our palms   and

as fingers moved, the harmony of words
absent of our reality
created a yellow rose...
as hands continued to be the wanderer
through empty sheets,
        I, woman
poet in violet solitude
            stood
        in this field
left a leaf of honey for the province behind me,
allowed my tears to become flower rings,
        continued crying
                for
    the lost poet in my nightly dreams...   continued

dreaming that you said
or I said
that your name was
at the far left corner
of my pocket
but you forgot
or I forgot
that I had no pockets...
it wasn't exactly your name I desired
but the way it could walk
down the ancient narrow streets
knowing it would die in a place it could grow again...
                                        again

I met
the old woodsman
still repeating, "always let the falcon rest
where it could see the east..."

       and I thought of her

berries grew on her nails,
her velvet hair calmed the air,
the temples of her unconscious mind not prepared
for the fatal cyclones...
the gods sent swans to guard the mansions
                                    in her eyes,
green muslin to cover the silky secrets of her
                                                skin,
                        of her delicate umbra...

                        and I thought of hands

that found their way around
winds of paper,
minds that remained hidden
even as they walked the crowded marketplace,
hearts that unlaced unlaced corsets
        ... being elsewhere...

III

Raspberry-colored stones turning around
the withering lighthouse, centuries of letters hiding
in the fleeing lanterns, shelves of long-lost books
whispering the birds' secrets
and
I
sitting
on the chariot of your last word,
wearing your only tunic,
holding the solitary pen
with my longing hands,
finally understanding
the shadow of your smile   understanding

that the orchard
allows souls to fantasize...
                    so
            I could continue riding on the yellow beret
toward the beehives
                        and the orchid colonies
continue believing
                    in the necklace of elephant gems
                            and the turquoise ballad
for I will always find
the end of the field which is its beginning...   the

beginning
    of a Lorcan play
in the middle of
       my life...

when "the night does not wish to come
so that you cannot come
and I cannot go."

so that the fantasia
continues
until the end of my life
       which is its beginning...   and

if everything migrates
even my body...
I know that in the yellow pond
your words
will find
the
exile's
key
and the petal that loves...   loves

the music trees in a lost afternoon, the kiss of a pale
face, the echo that will never pass until the deserts own
the moonlight, the dream the passers-by did not see
and
suffers for the table lost in a blurry lifeline, for dust's undefined
silhouettes crowding our villages...   and

I leave to come back...

colored jars releasing my jailed fist,
the river's dome telling me that we would
no longer be sheets flying to nowhere,
and I know
in the night of nights,
together
we will
listen
to the
water's voices...   voices

of distant shadows
sat beside me that afternoon in Paris...
the coffee's aroma
tricked me into deeper corners
and as coffee cups multiplied,
my ideas bounced back
like bullets I aimed at
                        myself...
more coffee...
                the doves settled inside of me...

it was the overture and the finale all at once
the composer's sonata
                        simply began...   all

began
all began
even before it started...

the poet caught by an ancient echo
held between the starting point
                    and
                              the
                                    final
                                          landing...

the poet hanging on my eyelashes, his words
falling like paint dripping on the book of my spirit.

and I continue loving
                              loving
fragments of him covering the honeycomb,
fragments of him hidden in the whitest beard...

the vine leaves cleanse my sight
as moistness settles in my eyes...

tonight, the night that will come...   come

to me with the wailing sea
                         and
                         the
                 intruder's armor.

come to me with the rosewater, the suffocating cans,
the damned objects, the blood stain on your friend's
shirt, the thyme leaves and the yellow raisins sitting in
your past, the pavilion of cypress trees, the land...

come
          or should I come to you
                                  and we shall go...
               to the dagger
                         and the silence
                                       silence

is when I lie on the hay's lap
and forget
moonlights I wanted to lose but couldn't...

I let my eyes follow the field
the field is everywhere
                    all at once...
I am in the never field
                    where it
never does not give...   give

.

us the field...

yellow branch
yellow field
yellow
I never saw more
I saw
     all
        at once...
             and

On March 13th

*"a great wonder appeared in the sky over Camelot. Two suns shone,
the like of which no one had seen before... Prepare for a great joy
and a great sorrow."*

on the thirteenth day of March
the birth of a poet,
the birth of new words
                              inside minds still unborn...
so we will prepare
prepare for all the suns
to gather around his poems
poems
that
will give us fire wings
and
allow
no tears in the kingdom...   poems

that are
behind the merchants' baskets,
in between the splinters,
on the woman's left breast,
in the field
                    all at once...   all

the windows continue to fly
as the field changes seasons...
at times the birds stop
to find a hat
and wonder
if the breeze
is lonely...   is

existence what you hide
in the lines of your hands but do not know...
know that the field
is the kiss
       and
    the desire
            all at once...
does the field
ever sleep without the field?

"Lovers think they're looking for each other,
but there's only one search: wandering
this world is wandering that, both inside one
transparent sky..."